POLICE TELEPHONE

FREE FOR
USE OF PUBLIC

ADVICE & ASSISTANCE
OBTAINABLE IMMEDIATELY

BBC CHILDREN'S BOOKS
UK | USA | Canada | Ireland | Australia
India | New Zealand | South Africa

BBC Children's Books are published by
Puffin Books, part of the Penguin
Random House group of companies
whose addresses can be found at
global.penguinrandomhouse.com.

www.penguin.co.uk
www.puffin.co.uk
www.ladybird.co.uk

 Penguin
Random House
UK

First published 2023
001

Written and designed by Paul Lang
Under Control/Into Control
written by Steve Cole
Art for Into Control by John Ross,
colouring by Alan Craddock

The authorized representative in the
EEA is Penguin Random House Ireland,
Morrison Chambers, 32 Nassau Street,
Dublin D02 YH68

Printed in Italy.

A CIP catalogue record for this book
is available from the British Library

ISBN: 978-1-405-95689-5

All correspondence to:
BBC Children's Books
Penguin Random House Children's
One Embassy Gardens,
8 Viaduct Gardens,
London SW11 7BW

CONTENTS

A LETTER FROM
THE DOCTOR

Dear reader,

Hello! Has it really been a whole year since I wrote to you last? Well, of course it has – this book is an annual; that's the whole idea, isn't it? Hope it's been a good year for you!

Mine's had its ups and downs. For example, I just died. Oh, it was beautiful. Clifftop, sunrise, arms outstretched, ready for whoever's coming next.

Y'see, death isn't the end for me. There's this thing I can do, a bit like holding in a sneeze for too long. When I finally let go, *bang*, I regenerate. New body, new face, new me. At least, that's what usually happens. But not this time.

Now I'm back in the TARDIS, wondering what the deal is with my teeth. First thing I did was run my tongue along them, just to see what I was dealing with, and noticed something unusually usual. They were my old teeth, from a few regenerations back!

Ooh, there's a custard-cream dispenser, I'd forgotten all about that – new braincells, y'see.

POLICE PUBLIC CALL BOX

POLICE TELEPHONE
FREE FOR
USE OF PUBLIC
ADVICE & ASSISTANCE
OBTAINABLE IMMEDIATELY
OFFICERS & CARS
RESPOND TO
URGENT CALLS
PULL TO OPEN

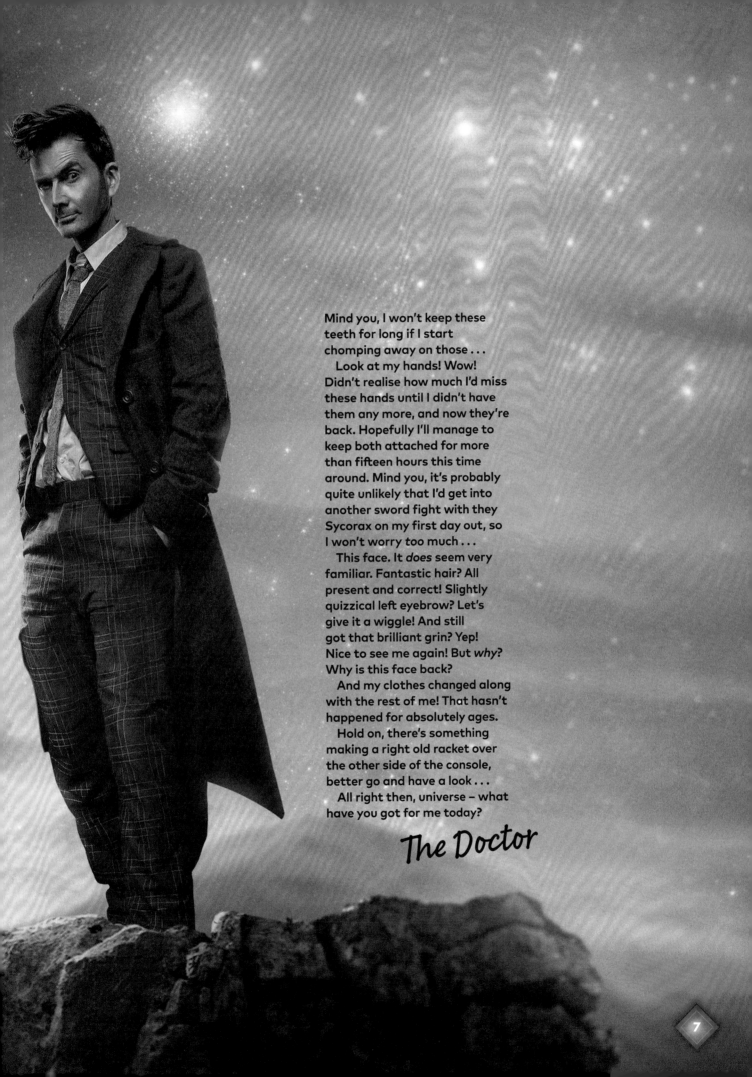

Mind you, I won't keep these teeth for long if I start chomping away on those . . .

Look at my hands! Wow! Didn't realise how much I'd miss these hands until I didn't have them any more, and now they're back. Hopefully I'll manage to keep both attached for more than fifteen hours this time around. Mind you, it's probably quite unlikely that I'd get into another sword fight with they Sycorax on my first day out, so I won't worry too much . . .

This face. It *does* seem very familiar. Fantastic hair? All present and correct! Slightly quizzical left eyebrow? Let's give it a wiggle! And still got that brilliant grin? Yep! Nice to see me again! But *why*? Why is this face back?

And my clothes changed along with the rest of me! That hasn't happened for absolutely ages.

Hold on, there's something making a right old racket over the other side of the console, better go and have a look . . .

All right then, universe – what have you got for me today?

The Doctor

WHAT? WHAT? WHAT? WHAT?

Meet the most amazing person in the history of the universe – the Doctor!

Everyone knows how stories work. They have a beginning, a middle and an ending. But what if your story is about the traveller in time and space called the Doctor? That's more complicated. The legend of the Doctor has been told and retold over the last sixty years, and they have had many different faces. That means numerous beginnings, multiple middles and endless endings!

THE SEVENTH DOCTOR
1987 - 1989, 1996
Played by Sylvester McCoy

THE NINTH DOCTOR
2005
Played by Christopher Eccleston

THE THIRD DOCTOR
1970 - 1974
Played by Jon Pertwee

THE FIFTH DOCTOR
1981 - 1984
Played by Peter Davison

THE FUGITIVE DOCTOR
2020 - 2022
Played by Jo Martin

THE THIRTEENTH DOCTOR
2017 - 2022
Played by Jodie Whittaker

THE EIGHTH DOCTOR
1996, 2013
Played by Paul McGann

For some, the story starts with the Timeless Child, discovered all alone beneath a wormhole to a faraway place. Others talk of an old man with white hair who stole a miraculous ship that could travel through time and space, then headed off to see what was out there.

People who have encountered the Doctor usually recall them arriving in an amazing blue box called the TARDIS along with one of their brilliant friends. These loyal companions have chosen to leave behind their old lives and discover everything the universe has to offer – good and bad!

But life on the TARDIS isn't all fun and adventure. Sometimes it goes to places full of terrifying creatures, including the Doctor's oldest and deadliest enemies – the Daleks!

THE ELEVENTH DOCTOR
2010 - 2013
Played by Matt Smith

THE FOURTH DOCTOR
1974 - 1981
Played by Tom Baker

THE FIRST DOCTOR
1963 - 1966
Played by William Hartnell

THE TWELFTH DOCTOR
2013 - 2017
Played by Peter Capaldi

THE TENTH DOCTOR
2005 - 2010
Played by David Tennant

THE WAR DOCTOR
2013
Played by John Hurt

THE SIXTH DOCTOR
1984 - 1986
Played by Colin Baker

THE SECOND DOCTOR
1966 - 1969
Played by Patrick Troughton

THE FOURTEENTH DOCTOR
2022 - 2023
Played by David Tennant

It doesn't really matter which part of this story you learn first, or what the Doctor looks like when when you join them – some things are always the same! Every Doctor does their best to battle monsters, help those in need and generally keep the universe ticking over, whether they're wearing a familiar old face or a brand-new one!

THE FIFTEENTH DOCTOR
2023 -
Played by Ncuti Gatwa

UNDER CONTROL

A BRAND-NEW ADVENTURE

BY STEVE COLE

'Whoa!' The Doctor burst out of the TARDIS and into a dank, rocky gloom. He grinned as he stared about. 'It's a cave. I love a cave!' The only dim light came from seams of gleaming silver in the stone. 'Natural phosphorescence? Or has someone given nature a hand? Or a claw, or a tentacle, or –?'

A scream, deep and despairing, echoed from somewhere in the blackness beyond the cave's mouth.

The Doctor's eyes widened. 'Someone to save, inside a cave.' He froze for a moment, every sense working to pinpoint the source of the scream. Then he set off at a sprint.

The cave opened on to a tunnel. Soft, silvery light blossomed over the bare rock

walls as the Doctor raced forward – was it responding to vibration? Movement? Body heat? The scream sounded again, more desperate this time, and the question was forgotten as he rounded a corner.

Ahead of him was a deep fissure in the rock. Wedged inside it was a powerful, white-furred creature easily twice his size. *A Strombok!* thought the Doctor. *Must have landed on Strombokkaccino.*

The Strombok's shaggy limbs were braced against the rock, its face twisted in effort.

The Doctor stared. 'Are you stuck?'

'Trapped.' The creature's groan was deep and rumbling.

'Let's have a look,' said the Doctor, darting straight into the fissure.

It was then that he realised the walls were closing in.

'Whoa! All right, then!' The Doctor added his strength to the Strombok's, making a concertina of his body between the two walls. 'Squeeze past me. Quickly!'

'No good.' Sweat was wetting the Strombok's furry face. 'Can't get out.'

'You can! Same way I got in.' The Doctor pulled his sonic screwdriver from inside his coat pocket and buzzed it about the crevice. There was some sort of technology in the rock walls, but he couldn't get a clear reading.

The Strombok groaned as rock dust showered down from above. 'Leave me.'

'Nah, don't want to do that. A-ha!' The Doctor pointed the sonic up at the ceiling. 'If I can hit just the right resonance where the wall meets the roof . . .' The pitch of the sonic snaked in and out of hearing, then hit a note so high even Time-Lord ears couldn't hear it. A huge slab of rock – very nearly the width of the fissure itself – started to detach itself from the ceiling overhead.

Yellow eyes bulged in the Strombok's face. 'We'll be flattened.'

'Not yet we won't!' The Doctor tugged down on the creature's right arm, dislodging it. Then with a grating, grinding sound, the unsupported wall closed inward – until it came up against one end of the slab of rock about to topple from the roof. With the rock wedged in place, the walls could no longer squeeze shut.

The Doctor dragged the Strombok out of the crevice, and they tumbled together to the cold ground. 'Now that we've rocked each other's world –' he said, panting for breath – 'why don't you tell me what's going on? I'm the Doctor. You are . . .?'

'Trapped.' The Strombok stared at him. 'Can't get out.'

'You are out.' The Doctor peered into the creature's clouded yellow eyes. 'But you might be in shock . . .'

There was another grating noise, and the slab of rock fell loose from the ceiling with a terrific *crump* as the walls now began to slide apart. The Strombok pushed the Doctor away and then scrambled back inside the widening fissure.

'Oi!' The Doctor stared as the Strombok disappeared through a gap in the rock at the back. Then, another, near-identical Strombok emerged from inside and stepped forward to stand in the same spot as his predecessor. The walls of the fissure began to shudder and close in again. This second Strombok flexed his arms mechanically, ready to brace against the wall.

The Doctor got up and crossed to the Strombok. 'Who's doing this to you? How many of you are in there?'

*

Suddenly, another scream of terror tore through the tunnel – this one higher pitched, almost bestial. The Doctor turned to his right and saw silvery glints sparkle along the length of the dark passage, like a trail of luminous breadcrumbs leading the way. He hesitated a moment, conflicted, as the Strombok grunted with the effort of holding back the vice of enclosing rock. But as more screams came from the same direction, he made the decision and ran off, yelling over his shoulder as he did so, 'I'll be back!'

The screams bounced off the rock in confusing echoes, and more than once the passageway branched into multiple tunnels leading in different directions. He let instinct guide him, and when he discovered a den of mole-like creatures, clustered and quivering together in a filthy cavern, the relief he felt was like a physical weight had been lifted from him. As the Doctor skidded to a stop, coattails flapping about his legs, he recognised three things at once: firstly, that the creatures had curved tusks for digging and wide, bulbous eyes for seeing in the dark, which could only mean they were a mining race from Vega Raptos. Secondly, the Vega Raptons seemed too terrified to have noticed his dramatic entrance. And thirdly, that the focus of their fear appeared to be a small pig.

'I'm the Doctor,' he announced. 'Who can tell me, are we on Strombokkaccino? The gravity feels off for Vega Raptos . . .' The miners ignored him, but the pig spared him a glance, and a morose oink. The Doctor approached it, making soothing noises. The pig shifted its meagre weight, skinny and sad looking – the Doctor noticed the poor thing had been roped to a nearby stalagmite. 'You're not so scary, are you?' the Doctor murmured. It looked to be a genuine Earthling pig, but as he reached out a hand to touch it, the Vega Raptons started screaming again.

'It will destroy you,' one shouted shrilly. 'Destroy us all.'

'Yeah?' The Doctor turned to face them. 'How's it gonna do that? I mean, you can never rule out a twist in the tail – not with a pig, anyway – but, still . . .'

'If we take our eyes off the beast, it will kill us,' a Vega Rapton said hoarsely. 'It will tear us apart.'

The Doctor stooped to untie the rope and scooped up the bony pig, which barely struggled. 'This poor animal's been too badly treated to do anything,' he said angrily. 'Look!'

'The armoured beast!' One of the miners was gibbering with fear, while its neighbours gouged at the rock in terror. 'Its bristles are tipped with poison; its tusks will tear your flesh . . .'

What are they seeing here? the Doctor wondered. With the pig under one arm, he scanned again with the sonic. And again, he picked up an unclear reading of technology somewhere in the walls that might not be technology at all.

The Doctor cast an accusing look at the sonic and pushed it back in his pocket. 'It's fine!' he told the Vega Raptons. 'Honestly.'

The Doctor backed away with the pig under his arm, holding up his free hand in a placating gesture. 'Look, I'm taking him away. You're free.'

But though the Vega Raptons quietened, they remained huddled together, tearful eyes still sharp and suspicious.

'Where is this place?' the Doctor asked. 'I've seen Stromboks, you lot and now a pig . . .'

'We travel to the place of offering,' someone said.

'Travel? To somewhere else in the caves, you mean? Where? I'll help you find it if you like.' There was no response, so the Doctor tried again. 'What place of offering? Offering what?'

'Ourselves,' came a whisper from the crowd.

The Doctor was about to question them further when he heard another hoarse scream from somewhere. 'Wait. Really?' He narrowed his eyes in sudden suspicion. 'Do you hear screams a lot around here?'

There was a rustling in the gloom as a hundred heads nodded.

'They travel with us,' someone said.

'Sounds like someone's in trouble,' the Doctor said. 'Who wants to help me help them?'

No one moved. The shouts started up again, multiple tones, and then the pig gave a short but plucky squeal.

'Come on then, Alfredo,' said the Doctor, disquieted. 'Can I call you Alfredo? Good name for a pig, probably. Anyway, let's leave this lot to it, shall we?' Alfredo didn't answer, but as the Doctor moved away with the pig in his arms, he wished that someone would. *What is happening here? Two wildly different races living side-by-side, trapped by their own fears. Two failed interventions. And now, a third species?* The Doctor felt a sense of urgency at the back of his mind, driving him to find whoever was in trouble.

That's who you are, he thought. *That's what you do – whatever you can.*

He paused for a moment to set down the pig. 'Nothing personal, Alfredo,' he apologised, 'I just don't know how dangerous it's gonna be through there and I might need both hands to . . .'

The Doctor trailed off as the pig scurried on ahead of him. 'Why do they never listen?' he muttered, and hurried after Alfredo.

Another cavern opened up to his right, lit with torches that burned infernal red. In the hellish light, people writhed helplessly on the floor, transfixed by a platform of stalactites with sharpened points which hung overhead. Alfredo snuffled up to one of the humans and licked his face. The man recoiled. 'What on Earth . . .?'

'Earth, is it?' the Doctor said. 'Well, sort of makes sense. Twenty light years on from Vega Raptos and maybe forty from Strombokkaccino. It's like a join the dots in space!'

'Christmas.' The man was staring at Alfredo. 'They came back for us at Christmas.'

'Christmas?' The Doctor frowned. 'Don't tell me the place of offering is Santa's grotto? Who came back for you?'

'They found the sword,' someone said.

'Found us,' said another.

'Whoever "they" are,' the Doctor replied, 'they're gonna find trouble. Who's with me?' He was unsurprised by the lack of response. 'Don't tell me – you'd rather lie on the ground feeling helpless . . .'

Alfredo nudged his ankle. The Doctor saw that the vicious spiked platform was held up by a heavy chain wrapped around a pulley. He studied it for a moment, then switched on the sonic. At the bright blue buzz, the chain jumped and unwound to its full extent. A collective scream went up from the humans as the stalactites dropped a half-metre lower, then stopped.

'That's as far as the trap can go,' the Doctor announced. 'Look. It's run out of chain.'

'You'll kill us all!' someone shouted. 'Get away from those controls.'

The Doctor waved the sonic and the chain rewound itself, hauling up the stalactites. With another buzz, they chuntered noisily free again, well away from their would-be victims. 'Not wanting to make you feel silly or anything, but you're not in any danger,' the Doctor insisted. 'I have a feeling the Stromboks' closing walls can't close all the way either, and Alfredo's no bother at all. But you're all being kept in a state of hypervigilance, focusing so much on your fear that you can't do anything about anything else. Come on, up you get.'

'You don't understand,' a man sneered.

'They'll spear us if we move away,' a woman said, 'and spare us if we don't.'

'Ahh, the mysterious "they" that you can't seem to name,' said the Doctor. 'Either you don't know, or it's some kind of hypnosis.' He blinked. 'They came back at Christmas. I wonder . . .'

A deep, rumbling bellow shook the ground and ploughed straight through his thoughts.

'Not again,' the Doctor sighed. 'Cue Doctor, off into the dark again, trusty pig by his side . . .'

But Alfredo had wandered off somewhere. The Doctor couldn't blame him – a strong reek of spice and decay was filling the corridor. He ran on towards it, aware of that same strange pressure at the back of his mind, trying to push him on. He stopped for a few moments, just to be sure he could resist the impulse, wary of a trap. But the sound of anyone in despair set his teeth on edge, and teeth were troubling enough at the best of times. He ran on along the tunnel . . . which ended in a huge circular chamber with six passages leading off from it. The chamber was dominated by a pool of dark fluid where vast octopods thrashed and quaked in a frenzy of motion.

'Sarnsquids!' The Doctor shook his head. On their native world, they were a gentle race of scientists and philosophers, their great bulk and clumsy appendages at odds with the elegance of their thought. 'What a menagerie . . .'

'The bile-pit burns!' shrieked one of the Sarnsquids, its single eye blood-red and rolling. 'Burns like fire!'

Of course, the Doctor realised. *The stench is the Sarnsquid's physical pain and fear.* 'What can I do?' he muttered. 'Got to be something . . .' A strong vibration hummed through the ground around the pool, and the Doctor saw the silver veins in the rock thread upwards like powerlines towards a giant porthole in the roof. Stars glowed beyond and, as he stared, gobsmacked, a pale ringed planet passed by.

The Doctor remembered the words of the Vega Rapton: *We travel.* 'This isn't just a cave system,' he breathed. 'It's a cave system inside a spaceship.' The howl of another Sarnsquid snapped him back into action. He waved the sonic around, tracing the silver powerlines. The same unclear readings showed that he was scanning something that either was or wasn't technology. The sensors he'd detected in the walls of the cells all fed into this arterial network. They reminded him of a humanoid nervous system pinned down in two dimensions – as if the Boneless were on board. But as the sonic did its work, these powerlines seemed to culminate in a decidedly three-dimensional crimson panel in the dark stone wall, where strange symbols danced and shook. The Doctor stabbed at the design with his fingers, directing the squiggles with short, precise movements until the panel cooled to blue and the thrashing of the Sarnsquids died down.

The Doctor crossed back to the edge of the giant pool and crouched down to address the octopods. 'I'm sorry. So sorry for what's been done to you.'

'Thank you.' A Sarnsquid reached out a quivering tentacle and pressed it to the Doctor's arm. 'The scale of our pain turns the psychic turbines that power this craft.'

'Yeah. Scream if you want to go faster,' the Doctor said grimly. 'The systems here were designed to torture whoever's in the pool in perpetuity. I shouldn't think there are many races who could withstand such a punishment.'

'No.' Another Sarnsquid panted, eyes closed. 'There are not many.'

'We are all slaves,' said another. 'Everyone on this vessel.

Slaves, to be brought to the place of offering,' the Doctor agreed. 'And I'm being brought there too . . .' He couldn't hear the Sarnsquids' response over a new clamour – hundreds of raucous cries and screams. *More people needing help, that's what I'm meant to think.* 'Turn the shouting up to eleven!' he yelled up at the ceiling. 'It's not gonna do you any good.' He walked out of the chamber through the nearest tunnel. The walls pulsed about him with thick red light. The atmosphere grew hot and oppressive. The Doctor heard groaning, keening, calling. Stromboks, Vega Raptons, humans, Sarnsquids. Other voices, taunting him with their pain. So many prisoners on this ship. He had to help them.

'Come on, then!' he yelled. 'Let's do this.' The Doctor marched on, spying light at the end of the tunnel ahead through the red haze. 'Who needs me most? Who needs help first?' He emerged into stone-cold whiteness, like a winter dawn, with a chill in the air to match. The ground was stained dark as if with blood. The screams fell silent. He stumbled to a stop, gazing around at a rocky arena.

'Well, now we know who really needs help,' he said. 'It's *me*.'

The story continues on page 48. But not as you might expect . . .

The greatest trick a Time Lord can pull off – cheating death!

SECRETS OF REGENERATION

WHAT IS REGENERATION?

For most living creatures, dying is the definitive ending of their story. The Doctor, however, is part of a race known as Time Lords, and they have an amazing gift that allows them to keep going. At the point of death, they throw out their arms to release an incredible burst of energy that renews every single cell in their body, and their life goes on. But not as it did before!

WARNING! There are two main ways a regeneration can go wrong: if a Time Lord is killed while it

NEW FACES

This regeneration energy doesn't just repair a Time Lord's body, it gives them a completely new one! Same person, different face, new teeth. In most cases, it's impossible to influence the outcome – young Time Lords can suddenly become old, and their gender is fluid.

MOOD SWINGS

But the change isn't just a physical one. A box-fresh Time Lord can also find that their personality is very different to before, which can be tough for them and their friends to come to terms with. The Doctors have all had their own distinct quirks, despite being the same person deep down.

STAND WELL BACK!

The Doctor's most spectacular regenerations

TRASHING THE TARDIS!

> I don't want to go!

THE SECRET

The Doctor always believed that regeneration was strictly a Time Lord secret, until discovering the ability had been stolen from a mysterious child found by a Gallifreyan explorer called Tecteun. But there was a bigger shock to come – this child (the Timeless Child) was the Doctor!

DESTROYING THE DALEKS!

> Regeneration number thirteen. We're breaking some serious science here, boys!

UNLUCKY THIRTEEN

Eternal life might seem like a great idea in theory, but the founders of Gallifreyan society realised it was more of a curse than a blessing. They decreed that each Time Lord should only be allowed to regenerate twelve times and live a maximum of thirteen lives (these twelve regenerations are called a 'regeneration cycle').

BEHIND THE SCENES

The concept of regeneration was cooked up when William Hartnell, who played the very first Doctor, became too ill to carry on in the role. That could have been the end, but the clever producers came up with the idea that the Doctor could renew his body when it wore out. And thank goodness they did, or you probably wouldn't be reading this book now!

EXPLOSIVE ENDING!

> Doctor, I let you go!

CLIFFTOP SUNRISE!

> Doctor Whoever-I'm-About-To-Be. Tag! You're it!

appening, or if they choose not to change. In both cases, it's game over!

17

RANDOM REGENERATIONS

The Master has tried to force every Doctor to regenerate at once and their faces have got muddled up. Can you identify all the Doctors and repair the timeline?

1
2
3
4
5
6
7
8
9
10
11
12
13
14
15
16

A
B
C
D

I
J
K
L

E
F
G
H

M
N
O
P

Turn to page 60 for the answers

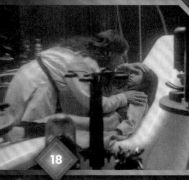

OUT OF CONTROL
The Doctor has been forced to regenerate several times. Tecteun made the Timeless Child regenerate to learn the secrets of the process.

The Master forced the Doctor to regenerate into a version with the Master's face and personality – he was trying to trash the real Doctor's reputation by doing evil deeds in her name!

By order of Article 412 of the Shadow Proclamation, we authorise the immediate apprehension of the following hostile forces:

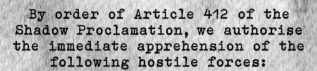

WANTED!

SUBJECT
DALEKS

PLANET OF ORIGIN
Skaro

WEAPONS
- Energy blaster
- Extendable sucker with optional claw attachment

FLEET
- Vast fleets of saucer-shaped spacecraft

AIMS
- To be the supreme creatures in the universe and destroy all beings they deem inferior.

KNOWN CRIMES
- Untold Time War crimes
- Invasion of a Level 5 planet
- Theft of 26 planets to create a Reality Bomb
- Time travel infractions

CURRENT STATUS
- Fleet devastated by multiple extinction events, but some units always survive. BE ON HIGH ALERT.

Protruding eye stalk

Twin luminosity dischargers

Energy weapon

Mutated organic creature inside

Multiple sensor globes

Reinforced Dalekanium casing

The Doctor's had many faces, but why does one in particular keep popping up?

THE STRANGE CASE OF THE SKINNY MAN

NEW FACES

Regeneration is usually a one-way process for a Time Lord. They gain a whole new body, and the old face becomes nothing more than a memory. But there's one set of teeth that keeps appearing in the Doctor's Time Lord timeline – the skinny one with a fondness for suits and sideburns.

EXTERMINATED

When the Doctor was caught by a blast of Dalek gunfire down one side of his body, it wasn't enough to kill him, although it did trigger a regeneration. However, this Doctor wasn't ready to say goodbye! He used just enough of the explosive *oomph* to heal his injuries, then fired the rest into a convenient bio-matching receptacle – the spare hand in the jar!

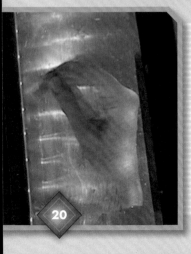

HANDY SPARE HAND

The first sign of something unusual about this Doctor came on the very first day of his life, during a swordfight on a Sycorax spaceship hovering above London. The Sycorax leader rudely chopped off the Doctor's right hand, sending it plummeting to the ground! Luckily, our hero had enough transforming energy left to grow a whole new one. He eventually found the original and kept it in a jar aboard the TARDIS.

METACRISIS!

The glowing goodness didn't stay safely stored for long, though. Donna Noble, trapped in the TARDIS and under heavy Dalek bombardment, heard a single heartbeat coming from the hand's jar and instinctively reached out to touch it. Wham! Instantaneous biological metacrisis. A whole new Doctor grew out of the spare hand.

ANOTHER DOCTOR

This Doctor looked exactly like the hand's original owner, but was quite different inside (thanks to a dose of Donna's human DNA – the heartbeat Donna heard was this Doctor's single heart, echoing through time). He'd also picked up Donna's impulsive personality! This combo made him too dangerous to be left wandering around, so the original Doctor packed his 'twin' off to a parallel universe to be guided by the incredible Rose Tyler.

THE DOCTORDONNA

Poor Donna didn't escape the metacrisis unharmed. She'd made the newly grown Doctor part-human, but he had returned the favour. Her head was now jam-packed with Time Lord knowledge – information it wasn't built to handle. The Doctor was forced to wipe every single memory of Donna's time with him, warning her family that if she ever recalled the skinny man in the brown suit, she would die.

BORN AGAIN

Other Doctors came and went, each very different from the last. Until one day, the Doctor stood on a clifftop awaiting the energy blast that would make everything new again. But this time, it wasn't a new Doctor who emerged after regeneration. The skinny man with the sideburns was back, with the same spiky hair as before!

THE

All the secrets of the Doctor's incredible ship . . .

Fancy a trip through time and space? Then you're going to need a TARDIS! The name stands for Time and Relative Dimension in Space, and the Doctor first acquired theirs by stealing it from the Time Lords' home planet of Gallifrey.

Back then it was in its default skin, which meant it was just an unassuming grey cylinder. But that's where the magic begins. Every TARDIS is equipped with a chameleon circuit, meaning the outside can take on a different form to blend in every time it lands somewhere new.

Like its owner, the TARDIS isn't a big fan of fading into the background, and has stubbornly stuck in the form of a blue Police Box ever since a stop-off in 1960s London.

The Doctor once landed a different TARDIS on Earth and it turned itself into a house!

TARDIS FACT!

The Doctor and friends can understand the languages they hear wherever they go because the TARDIS translates for them.

ON THE OUTSIDE

The TARDIS appears to love being a big, blue box – but there have been subtle upgrades over the millennia . . .

TARDIS INSIDE OUT

ON THE INSIDE

The first thing most people notice about the inside of the TARDIS is that it's much bigger than the outside. The Doctor's usually vague about how this can even be possible, but it's something to do with the inside and outside being tethered together between different dimensions.

TARDIS FACT!
Why does the console have six sides? Because it's supposed to have six pilots!

When the Doctor set off on his travels, the TARDIS had a gleaming white control room covered with dials and switches, and a magnificent six-sided control console right in the middle. At the centre of this console sits the time rotor, a column connected to the engines below that moves up and down when the TARDIS is in flight.

The TARDIS has been known to redecorate itself, in keeping with the Doctor's changing styles. But the basic layout always remains the same. The controls might look different, yet the Doctor always seems to know what each one does.

TARDIS FACT!
There are loads of rooms leading off the main one – including a swimming pool!

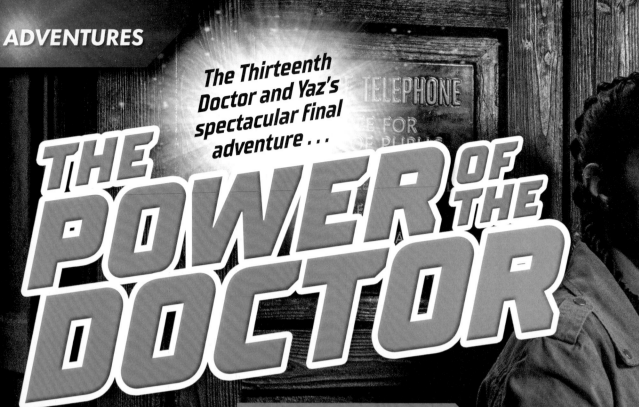

The Thirteenth Doctor and Yaz's spectacular final adventure . . .

THE POWER OF THE DOCTOR

CYBER BATTLE

There's no such thing as a quiet day for the Doctor, but some are just that bit more chaotic than others. This particular day kicked off with a CyberMaster assault on a super-fast space train, a rogue Dalek getting in touch with information about a plan to destroy the human race, and the Doctor's friend Dan deciding it was time to stop travelling in the TARDIS.

THE LAST DAY

The Doctor's old companions, Ace and Tegan, teamed up with Kate Stewart from UNIT to investigate the appearance of bearded Russian monk Rasputin's face on some famous paintings. It turned out the face wasn't Rasputin's – it was the Master's. And he had a stark warning for the Doctor: 'This is the day you die!'

EARTH SHOCK

What the double-crossing Dalek hadn't mentioned was that its race had teamed up with the CyberMasters, and the Master himself. Their evil scheme was to cause every volcano on Earth to erupt at the same time. The ultimate game of Floor is Lava!

FORCED FACE SWAP

But the Master had an even more cruel fate in store for the Doctor. He planned to make her go through a forced regeneration into him, so he could head out across time and space to trash the Doctor's reputation forever. Once the swap was complete, the Master had become the Doctor, much to Yaz's horror. She vowed she'd never accept him.

HOLO HELPER

With the real Doctor out of action, she created a hologram version of themselves and sent it out to help Ace and Tegan deal with the Daleks and Cybermen. The Doctor's friends then captured the Master and made him undo the forced regeneration. But he was furious at being defeated, and declared that if he couldn't be the Doctor, then neither could she.

OLD FACES

Meanwhile the Doctor found herself at the Edge of Existence – part of her own mind that she passes through just before regenerating. There, she met the Guardians of the Edge, who looked suspiciously like some of her older regenerations! The Guardians told her the forced regeneration could be reversed.

POLICE PUBLIC CALL BOX

THE FINAL JOURNEY

The Master then channelled a massive energy beam at the Doctor, mortally wounding her and causing her next regeneration to begin. Yaz managed to carry the Doctor back to the TARDIS, and the two of them went on one last, bittersweet trip. It would soon be time to say goodbye . . .

DEADLY DIAMOND

It's the Diamond Anniversary of Doctor Who, which means the Doctor is celebrating 60 years of adventures. That adds up to a lot of enemies over the years! Help the Ood find all 60 horrors lurking in the diamond . . .

Turn to page 60 for the answers

```
                    S
                  F I D
                F D L S N
              V A V E K G A
            J W M T N I J W C
          T V S K S C T A G H L
        D V F Z W U E H P S E C Y
      N G U F V D A V R O S A S Y Y
    T I L P V S N X R A G V V S A B S
  Q R M H F U G Y V Z M D F E H Y D E U
A V K I N Z G Z I Y G H M T N W C Q N R C
D H B J N B D Q U Z J G R P M L U K N S L M L
N G T B A J D B Q D E L O H F Z Y G O N O W P A V
P U R C P D X F E O L X F X L K X H K K K R T G E N L
H D E M N N I M O N Z N I O P Y H S O V G Y I T N M Q D O
J V P U M M R B Q D N M P S P Z V E O S X O V T I S E A N I K
F N A B H O N A N N P W S D E Z U C A N T C Z N E V J U G L B F T
K P E P W D R I K R M H E S K M J V W I T R D I M E Q H U A D I E F E
W S R R V K C A V S K A V X S Q P J K Y F A B R J E V T I R B L F G O A R
M A I A B V H R X H A D N F F M X T S I L C R Q H Q U H Z C M T U P Z O M W I
M E Q V A H H B R K H G C D J X O L Y U M H E A D O J G R A N D S E R P E N T U L
I S Y L T J Y C K D N V Y Y R W N H M C N O E H N U J Z Z M O E L F S Q P A W D V J E
V J G X C Y C L P G R O J X Q E U Q X E H A E K F T H E M E E P O M V B D M G A K B P M P
J W G A S A B Z O R B A L O F F L A X W X I U J P U G H S E W K S M I L E R M H E K C P E B T
G P X B Z K Q N Z S H O R N W G M P M S S L L N T K K N S Y Y S Z T E S H A L S L E G G U X U E I
W G S Q Z U H I C E W A R R I O R J A N S E V D K F A E G C U I Z Z R M Q W O A A L B N Q Z L V Q T L
I W R A R T H W A R R I O R L N T B S G K Q M C O Z T L F A R F Y I A I M Y D R N A M I R E I S K
J C R E T U M E O A X Q S O N F D N T A N D Z R Q W Y O V R E Q T K N B U Y W S K H T R G D O
U C S Y C O R A X N J H K O U A G G E A L N E R Q T Z A E R U O S P F P C U P N V R N D Y
H Z Q X H T N O N U I H E G M Q E R R C V T J B P C C X C I V T E T R A P U F O I O U
D N P U V T K F G S S N Q P H D H M N F O U O V M M T K Z O D F V N S I Q P T O T
O C R U B H A A Q I T N T L S G A J F L O O D C J L U C R N R P D S Y C P C E
L A S W L A Q P O R I E I O L Q F W D X U I C E F C T E Z I Y S A Z N Q H
E X A S X E Q M L N Y U N A K E B K A S A A V I N B R M F T A N L M T
L O T E O M S W G M B L Z V A T R A X I S E K Q U R U N X E D Y C
D W U H L O M P L Q E M L N Q X E A D I P O S E Y C M T S R N
O F T Z S V B T U X A H W M S Y K S G A O J A Y M V U M A
S Q K R H O I X E T Y I Q O C F J N K S I D J Z N F I
T L W A S R J T H I J A R I A N Z G L Q N E N S R
O K X Y C E Q U Y Z K B J I H A U P Z N Y R U
C E Y G F B V A S H T A N E R A D A L U L
L U W X E J N S E A D E V I L T H K I
A S Z O M F V G U I A C R I W L S
F O E X Y N Q H P D Y L S H L
A X H J U D O O N L G G Z
N V P Y M Y Q I G X K
E K Y W K R E F F
X Y G K R S R
V W D I D
Z J L
G
```

Tick them off as you find them . . .

- ABZORBALOFF
- ADIPOSE
- ASHAD
- ATRAXI
- AUTON
- AXON
- AZURE
- CARRIONITE
- CYBERMAN
- DALEK
- DAVROS
- DREG
- DRYAD
- ELDRAD
- EMPTY CHILD
- FLOOD
- FORETOLD
- GELTH
- GRAND SERPENT
- HAEMOVORE
- HEAVENLY HOST
- ICE WARRIOR
- JUDOON
- KASAAVIN
- KRILLITANE
- LADY CASSANDRA
- MACRA
- MANDREL
- MARA
- MASTER
- MIRE
- MORAX
- NIMON
- OOD
- PTING
- QURUNX
- REAPER
- RIBBONS
- SEA DEVIL
- SENSORITE
- SIL
- SILENCE
- SILURIAN
- SKITHRA
- SLITHEEN
- SMILER
- SONTARAN
- SWARM
- SYCORAX
- TERILEPTIL
- TETRAP
- THE MEEP
- THIJARIAN
- TOCLAFANE
- TRITOVORE
- VASHTA NERADA
- VESPIFORM
- WEEPING ANGEL
- WRARTH WARRIOR
- ZYGON

By order of Article 412 of the Shadow Proclamation, we authorise the immediate apprehension of the following hostile forces:

WANTED!

SUBJECT
CYBERMEN

PLANETS OF ORIGIN
Mondas, Earth, Gallifrey

WEAPONS
- Wrist-mounted laser blasters
- Electrical pulses from hands

FLEET
- Cybercarriers
- Colony ships

AIMS
- To achieve victory in the Cyber-wars
- To convert all organic creatures to Cybermen

KNOWN CRIMES
- Assisting destruction of the Time Lord race
- Attack on headquarters of an allied organisation (UNIT)
- Unauthorised upgrading of unwilling life forms.

CURRENT STATUS
- Cyber Warrior battalions now enhanced by evolved CyberMasters. WARNING - THESE UNITS HAVE THE ABILITY TO REGENERATE!

Wrist weapons

Distinctive metal handles on helmet

Life support unit on chest

Humanoid shape with metallic upgrades

Spikes along limbs

BACK IN BUSINESS

The Doctor and Donna are together again . . .

'SOMETIMES I THINK THERE'S **SOMETHING MISSING**. LIKE I HAD SOMETHING **LOVELY**, AND IT'S **GONE**.'

'I DON'T BELIEVE IN **DESTINY**, BUT IF DESTINY EXISTS, IT IS **HEADING FOR DONNA NOBLE**'

'THE SHOW IS JUST **BEGINNING**! WORLDWIDE **PREMIERE**!'

'IF SHE EVER **REMEMBERS ME,** SHE WILL **DIE!**'

SPECIAL 1
THE STAR BEAST

SPECIAL 2
WILD BLUE YONDER

SPECIAL 3
THE GIGGLE

FIRST DAY
of the Doctor

The Doctor shares a selection of diaries from their debut adventures . . .

THE SEVENTH DOCTOR

There I was, in the middle of a spin class (courtesy of my friend Mel), when a tumultuous time storm stole the TARDIS mid-flight and dropped it on the planet Lakertya, causing me to regenerate following a bumpy crash-landing. After much confusion involving a curly ginger wig, I eventually identified my assailant as the Rani – an old schoolmate who had gone rogue and was feeding geniuses into a giant brain as part of some preposterous plan. She wanted to achieve time manipulation on a grand scale, and I wanted to stop her. I'm sure I don't need to tell you who got their way!

THE TENTH DOCTOR

Oh, I remember, it was Christmas, wasn't it? I love Christmas, I wish it could be Christmas every day. There's a town called Christmas, I must go there some time, then it really would be Christmas every day. Anyway, where was I? Oh yeah, I was on the Powell Estate having a nice nap after my regeneration when a ship packed with Sycorax appeared above London. My friend Rose Tyler did her best to keep things under control, but what you really need when something like that happens is a Doctor: me! One nice cup of tea later and I'd sent the Sycorax packing with just a well-aimed satsuma, all in time for turkey and stuffing courtesy of Rose's mum, Jackie. I also found a great suit that day which I plan to wear for a long time. Hope I don't manage to get it all raggedy . . .

THE THIRTEENTH DOCTOR

The last thing you want to deal with while you're wearing in a new pair of feet is a Stenza warrior who's come to Earth on a hunting expedition. But that's exactly the situation I found myself in, first day on the job. Fortunately, I had help from some incredible people – Ryan, Yaz and Graham, my new fam. You could even say they were fam-tastic! You're right, sorry, never saying 'fam-tastic' again. This Stenza bloke, Tim Shaw, had teeth embedded all over his face. One of MY old faces was obsessed with his teeth, so he'd have loved Tim! I'll never forget that we lost the amazing Grace, Ryan's gran and Graham's wife, that day. She'd have been brilliant in the TARDIS.

THE TWELFTH DOCTOR

Look, all I'm saying is that if you'd just regenerated, found yourself immediately swallowed up by a rampaging dinosaur, galloped about on a horse for a bit, nearly been harvested for your flesh and organs, fought a robot with half a face in a hot-air balloon made out of human skin, AND had to deal with whatever trouble Madame Vastra and her friends were involved in, maybe you wouldn't have the usual big, daft grin on your face either.

THE FIFTEENTH DOCTOR

'What the h[...] here?' are [...] first word[...] saying t[...] Ruby S[...] other [...] some [...] adv[...]

My first day as the Doctor

What if the Doctor regenerated into you? Amazing, right? But how would your first day on the job go?

I would wear:

My companion would be called:

And this is their story:

The first monster I'd meet would be:

And I'd defeat them by:

The inside of my TARDIS would look like this:

MONSTER

The Doctor's two most terrifying enemies have had their own glow-ups over the years . . .

DALEKS

The Daleks were the very first alien creatures seen in *Doctor Who*, sixty years ago! They were designed by Raymond Cusick, who came up with the iconic shape that's still used today.

These days it takes three people to bring a Dalek to life: one in the casing propelling with foot power and moving the sucker and gun, another operating the head and eyestalk by remote control, and a third shouting 'Exterminate' into a special microphone!

Raymond's original idea was to have a man riding a small tricycle inside each Dalek. That was too fiddly, so the operators ended up on a little seat, using their own feet to move the Dalek around.

Jodie Whittaker's Thirteenth Doctor was the first to face a fully robotic Dalek - these models didn't have a pilot inside!

EVOLUTION OF THE DALEKS

REGENERATIONS

CYBERMEN

The original Cybermen were created in 1966 by costume designer Sandra Reid. The first designs had creepy cloth faces with an assortment of metal parts attached.

They've been upgraded many times, but mostly keep a similar shiny, silver look.

Ashad was a partly converted Cyberman whose human face was still visible. The art team sculpted the costume design for the actor's head so that it would be a perfect fit for him.

It's hard work playing a Cyberman because the costume is very bulky and it's hot inside, so the actors need regular breaks to keep cool.

The most recent Cybermen were a mix of Time Lord and Cyberman design – instead of the famous handles on top of their heads, they had elegant detailing based on the fancy collars worn by Time Lords.

EVOLUTION OF THE CYBERMEN

Donna's back – and she's not alone!

WE ARE FAMILY

DONNA

Donna Noble – a big-mouthed temp with a heart of gold from Chiswick in West London – thought she knew exactly where her life was going as she walked down the aisle on her wedding day. She'd met the man of her dreams and was looking forward to married life. Then everything began to go wrong.

For a start, she vanished from the church halfway to the altar, and instead found herself standing in the TARDIS, staring at a baffled Doctor. Also, her husband-to-be was secretly betraying her by plotting with a giant red spider woman to let her spider babies feast on the population of Earth. Major red flag!

After all that was sorted, Donna was so weirded out that she declined the Doctor's offer to show her the universe. But once he was long gone, she couldn't stop thinking about the amazing life she had turned down, and began searching for the mysterious traveller and his blue box . . .

Reunited, the Doctor and Donna became the best of friends. But as they went about their adventures, the Doctor came to realise that

SYLVIA

Donna's mum barely batted an eyelid when her daughter vanished into thin air on the day of her first wedding – she was already weary from years of Donna's silly stunts. Sylvia was always suspicious of the Doctor whenever he turned up, as chaos was never far behind, and she was furious to learn Donna had been off wandering through the stars with him. Knowing that Donna could die if she remembers her time with the Doctor, she's frantic with worry when he reappears after so many years.

SHAUN

It was second time lucky for Donna when she finally made it all the way up the aisle to wed Shaun Temple, a kind man who wasn't plotting with a spider woman behind her back. The pair didn't have much money but were still happy together – although a winning lottery ticket (a wedding present from the Doctor) looks to have changed that!

WILF

Wilfred Mott is Donna's grandad – a brave old soldier who stepped up to help the Doctor after Donna lost her memories. When the Master tried to turn every human on Earth into a copy of himself, Wilf went into battle to stop him. He even manned a laser-blasting cannon aboard a spaceship! Wise Wilf was never phased by the Doctor or the many aliens who always follow in his wake. He thought mankind's destiny was to reach for the stars and get along with the people they found there.

ROSE

Rose is Donna and Shaun's daughter, whose life changes when she stumbles upon something alien, just like her mum did! But if Donna can't remember the Doctor, how did Rose end up with the same name as one of their old friends? One thing's for certain – the world was never quite the same for this seemingly ordinary family after they first crossed paths with the Doctor. And now he's back – in a big way!

Donna might be more than just an ordinary woman. In fact, she could even be the most important person in all of creation.

That's because Donna's destiny was to save our universe – and every other universe out there – from the destruction caused by a Dalek weapon called the Reality Bomb. After she accidentally caused a two-way biological metacrisis, she was flooded with Time Lord DNA, giving her the skills and knowledge to defeat Davros, creator of the Daleks.

Sadly, this victory came at a price. Donna had to give up her memories of the Doctor, and the amazing life they'd had together. Now, years later, she still has a strange sense that there was once more to her life than she remembers.

SUPER

The Doctor never carries a weapon, just a trusty sonic screwdriver...

The Second Doctor

The very first sonic screwdriver we saw the Doctor use was the most basic model of all – it looked more like a smart silver pen than a screwdriver.

The Third, Fourth and Fifth Doctors

This flashy silver design originally had yellow stripes and an electric toothbrush-style head. Don't clean your gnashers with it though – they'll vibrate right out of your head!

The Eighth Doctor

When the Doctor's sonic was destroyed it took him a few hundred years to replace it. This Doctor opted for a similar model, with a glowing red light at the top.

The Thirteenth Doctor

Stuck on Earth with no access to the TARDIS, the newly regenerated Doctor had to build the next sonic screwdriver by hand! It was forged from local Sheffield steel, with all sorts of old junk welded, glued and soldered on.

The Ninth and Tenth Doctors

The next upgrade had an organic, coral texture that matched how the TARDIS looked at the time, with a blue light at the top. It was supercharged, so the Doctor used it more!

The Eleventh and Twelfth Doctors

By now, the TARDIS was able to whip up replacement sonic screwdrivers on demand! This model could be controlled by just *thinking* of a function.

The Twelfth Doctor's second model

After trying out wearable tech, the Doctor turned back to his traditional screwdriver, which now had impressive light modes and movements.

SONIC

Primary sonic emitter

The Fourteenth Doctor

A new screwdriver for a new Doctor, with some familiar elements!

Guns? Warships? Killer lasers? The Doctor only needs their brainpower to get out of a tricky spot. But sometimes even a Time Lord needs a helping hand! That's where the sonic screwdriver comes in. This multipurpose marvel can do all kinds of astonishing stuff – everything from scanning and diagnostics to unlocking doors and disabling weapons. And yes, it can even be used for unscrewing screws (although not always, as it doesn't work on wood).

Central sonic cluster

Wide area dispersal petals

Activation button

Function access controls

Resonator cage

Frequency and intensity dials

SONIC FACTS

● After getting bored of the sonic screwdriver, the Doctor once swapped it for a pair of sonic sunglasses.

● The Doctor made a sonic lipstick for his old friend Sarah Jane Smith.

● The sonic screwdriver can't be used as a weapon, but the Master once built a very nasty laser screwdriver that could.

DESIGN A NEW SONIC SCREWDRIVER

There's a new Doctor coming, and he's going to need his very own sonic screwdriver. But he wants your help to design it!

This sonic screwdriver's top three features are:

1 ....

2 ....

3 ....

The one thing it can't do is:

....

....

It's made from:

....

....

VREEEEEEEEE

By order of Article 412 of the Shadow Proclamation, we authorise the immediate apprehension of the following hostile forces:

WANTED!

SUBJECT
WEEPING ANGELS

PLANET OF ORIGIN
Unknown

WEAPONS
- Exceptional physical strength
- Psychic manipulation
- Power to transform others into an Angel

FLEET
- None – self-transporting

AIMS
- To feast on the time energy of their victims by sending them into the past

KNOWN CRIMES
- Illegal extraction of potential energy
- Assisting the Time Lord agency, Division
- Misuse of psychic powers
- Petrification of inhabited victims

CURRENT STATUS
- Still active throughout the universe in ALL time periods.

Grey statues with wings

Look into an Angel's eyes for long enough and another will grow inside you

Angelic face that turns feral when attacking

Turn to stone when quantum locked to defend themselves

Super-fast movement in the blink of an eye

Think all Time Lords are as brave and brilliant as the Doctor? Think again!

TERRIBLE

THE TIME LORDS OF GALLIFREY

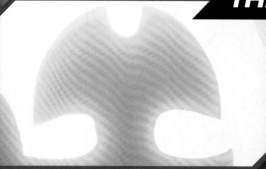

For a long time, it was a mystery as to why the Doctor had deserted their home planet in favour of roaming the universe. But once they started meeting Time Lords and visiting Gallifrey more often, the reason soon became clear. Their own people were awful! Corrupt, backstabbing, interfering and occasionally just plain evil – sometimes the Time Lords can be the worst enemies of all . . .

THE MONK

WHO WAS HE?
The first rogue Time Lord the Doctor met, he turned up on Earth in 1066 pretending to be a monk.

WHAT HAPPENED?
His real aim was to change the course of the planet's history by altering the outcome of the legendary Battle of Hastings, so the Doctor had to make sure events went ahead as planned!

OMEGA

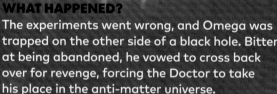

WHO WAS HE?
One of the founders of Time Lord society, Omega was a brilliant engineer working to discover the secrets of time travel by harnessing the power of a supernova.

WHAT HAPPENED?
The experiments went wrong, and Omega was trapped on the other side of a black hole. Bitter at being abandoned, he vowed to cross back over for revenge, forcing the Doctor to take his place in the anti-matter universe.

RASSILON

WHO WAS HE?
That depends on who you ask! Some remember him as a visionary leader, while others say he was a wicked tyrant.

WHAT HAPPENED?
The Time Lords resurrected their long-dead Lord President to lead them in battle against the Daleks in the Time War. The Doctor put a stop to his ultimate plan, which was to destroy the universe and leave only the Time Lords in existence, as creatures of pure thought. Realising that Rassilon was as bad as the Daleks, the Doctor exiled him from Gallifrey. forever.

THE RANI

WHO WAS SHE?
A rogue Time Lord banished for her unethical scientific experiments.

WHAT HAPPENED?
The wicked Rani enslaved an entire planet and had the bright idea of removing the people's ability to sleep so they could work harder. Without sleep, the people turned nasty, so she travelled to Earth to steal a crucial sleep chemical from humans – but her experiment was shut down by the Doctor.

TIME LORDS

THE YOUNG MASTER

The Doctor and the Master met at school, where they took part in a Time Lord initiation ceremony by looking into the Time Vortex. Some would be inspired, some would run away, and others would go mad . . .

THE CHARMING MASTER

The Master's appearance and personality often mirror the Doctor's, and this version was as courteous as his counterpart. But don't be fooled; he was still a cold-blooded killer working with aliens to help them conquer Earth.

THE FRAZZLED MASTER

The Doctor saw the Master again when he was nearing the end of his final life. Unable to regenerate, his body was in a terrible state – a living skeleton with a few remaining scraps of skin stretched over it.

THE BODYSNATCHING MASTER

With a new body out of the question, the Master was forced to take desperate action by stealing one. He didn't treat it very well, subjecting it to shrinking, burning and even being slowly turned into a cheetah!

THE MANY FACES OF THE MASTER

The Master is probably the most terrible of all the Time Lords, and like his arch enemy, the Doctor, he's been through a few different regenerations . . .

THE HIDDEN MASTER

The cowardly Master opted out of the Time War by using a Chameleon Arch to disguise himself as a human baby. This baby grew up to be Professor Yana, a kindly scientist whose evil essence was locked away in his pocket watch.

THE PRIME MASTER

Meeting the Doctor again triggered Yana's memories, and the Master was back, disguised as Harold Saxon, the UK's Prime Minister. He was tormented by a drumming sound planted in his head by the Time Lords.

THE MISTRESS

The next Master was different – she looked like a woman and called herself Missy! At first, it seemed as if this version would be as evil as all the others, but Missy showed signs of wanting to be a better person, full of remorse for all the deaths she'd caused.

THE DESTRUCTIVE MASTER

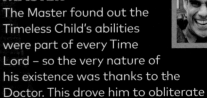

The Master found out the Timeless Child's abilities were part of every Time Lord – so the very nature of his existence was thanks to the Doctor. This drove him to obliterate Gallifrey and all the Time Lords.

TIME LORD STYLE

Clothes maketh the Time Lord, and the Doctor's been perfectly turned out to match every personality . . .

A fancy-looking fella in frilly shirts who was rarely without a cape for swooshing around.

This cheeky chap's mop-top was the perfect complement to a baggier, clownish style.

The first Doctor we met was a real old-fashioned gent, with formal clothes to match. Check out the fancy bow tie!

Following a visit from this Doctor and his very bright coat, some parts of the galaxy report a spike in sales of protective sunglasses.

When you're trying to give off an air of mystery, a jumper covered in question marks is the only way to go.

Dressed for a game of cricket, and rocking a stick of celery on his jacket? Bold!

Thick, curly hair pairs well with a multicoloured scarf.

Bow ties are cool!

This outfit started out smart but ended up wartorn. The Doctor later added a bandolier – a crossbody belt for holding weapons or ammo.

Keeping things simple with a leather jacket and jumper. Good for maintaining a low profile.

An iconic look featuring a striped brown suit and scruffy sneakers. This Doctor sometimes switched things up by swapping the shirt and tie for a T-shirt.

A stylish navy coat with red lining that looked just as good with a crisp, white shirt or a comfy hoodie.

The Doctor ended up wearing a mash-up of her old outfits as a result of one of the Master's diabolical schemes. Can you spot which bits are which?

WHO'S HATS!

The Doctor's best headgear

STOVEPIPE

PANAMA

TAM O'SHANTER

FEZ

STRAW

DEERSTALKER

Charity-shop chic! This Doctor's coat was a statement that could be seen from space – and beyond. Perfect to pair with a rainbow-striped top.

Wait, this one seems familiar. And how did the Doctor's clothes manage to regenerate too?

DOUBLE DANGER

There's been a rupture in time and the Doctor needs to know which eight squares show what's changed between two realities. Can you spot the crucial differences between these pictures and help to save the day?

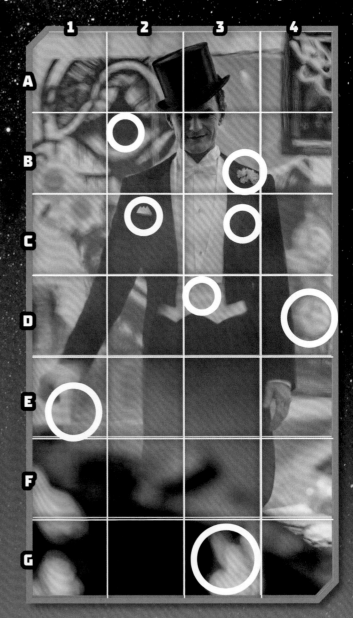

Write your answers here. The First one is already filled in to start you off.

Turn to page 60 for the answers

 1 D3
 2
 3
 4
 5
 6
 7
 8

WANTED!

SUBJECT
SONTARANS

PLANET OF ORIGIN
Sontar

WEAPONS
- Rheon carbine swagger sticks
- Explosives
- Laser guns

FLEET
- Claw-shaped motherships
- Spherical single-occupant ships

AIMS
- To conquer! Sontarans are obsessed with war and will fight almost anyone over almost anything

KNOWN CRIMES
- Invasion of Gallifrey
- Unsanctioned time travel
- Attempted poisoning of Earth
- Exploiting the Flux to wage war across multiple worlds and time periods

CURRENT STATUS
- Sontaran fleet wiped out by the Flux event but more clones are being produced all the time.

Probic vent on back of neck to feed on energy

Rounded head

Battle armour

Almost identical clones

Two fingers and a thumb on each hand

THE REGENERATION

Uh-oh – you've both started glowing! But there's only enough regeneration energy for one of you to change. Whoever makes it to the Regeneration Zone first is the winner, and gets to be the next Doctor!

5
A Sycorax warrior chops off your pinkie. *GO BACK TO 3 AND GROW A NEW ONE.*

6

15

4

3

7
Your old body's wearing a bit thin. *MISS A TURN* for a snooze.

14
The TARDIS redecorates itself! *GO TO 19 FOR A LOOK.*

2
You regenerate but keep your old face. *YOUR OPPONENT MISSES A TURN.*

8

16

1
START HERE

9
You're mid-regeneration and recognise your old teeth. *SKIP TO 21.*

13

17

10

12
A giant spider chases you back 6 spaces. *GO TO 6.*

18
You're blasted by River Song while regenerating. *GAME OVER.*

11

19

YOU

20
The Time Lords give you a new cycle of lives. *THROW AGAIN.*

22

21
Your explosive energy damages the TARDIS. *GO BACK TO START*

GAME

A game for two players

5

4 Your clothes regenerate with you, and you look great! *STRUT TO 15.*

3

6

2 You get stuck in the town of Christmas for 900 years. *MISS A TURN.*

15

7

16 Leftover energy flows into your handy spare hand. *GO BACK TO 9.*

14 You have a new head and you're finally ginger! *GO TO 20.*

8 Metacrisis means there are now two of you. *YOUR OPPONENT MISSES A TURN.*

9

1 START HERE

17

13

12 You drop the sonic while falling out of the TARDIS. *GO BACK TO 7* to look for it!

10 You meet a version of yourself you'd forgotten about. *THROW AGAIN.*

18 Tecteun steals your secret of regeneration. *GO BACK TO START.*

19

11

WIN

22 The Master forces you to regenerate into him. *GAME OVER.*

20

21

YOU WILL NEED

- Dice
- Some coins or counters
- Bucketloads of regeneration energy
- A bit of luck!

47

INTO CONTROL

SYCORAX! SHOULD'VE KNOWN.

SYCORAX STRONG!

SYCORAX MIGHTY!

SYCORAX **ROCK!**

SYCORAX OUGHT TO KNOW BETTER! ABDUCTION, BLOOD RITES, SLAVERY...

NOT HAVING THAT FOR A SECON NOW, WHO'S IN CHARGE HERE?

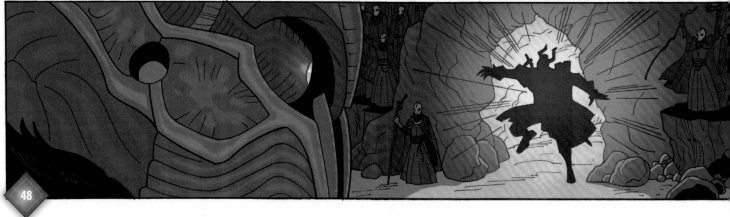

BLOOD CONTROL? YOU THOUGHT YOU COULD USE THAT OLD TRICK ON ME?

YOUR BODY AND SOUL BELONG TO THE SYCORAX. YOU HAVE COME TO US AT A USEFUL TIME.

OI!

FZZZZZZZ...

I'VE ALREADY CLOCKED WHAT YOU'RE DOING HERE. YOU HAVE THE FASTEST, CLEANEST SHIP PROPULSION SYSTEMS. AND THE MOST HORRIBLE.

WE STRIDE THE LONG DARKNESS. OUR SUPPLY OF FUEL MUST BE INEXHAUSTIBLE.

PAIN INTO PROPULSION. BUT THESE SARNSQUID ARE HALF-DEAD WITH EFFORT.

THERE ARE NOT MANY RACES WHO COULD WITHSTAND SUCH A PUNISHMENT. HOWEVER . . . A TIME LORD . . .

YOU WANT TO USE ME?

BLOOD CONTROL CANNOT COMPEL OTHERS TO ACT CONTRARY TO THEIR SPIRIT. BUT YOU WISH TO HELP THE HELPLESS, RESCUE THE WEAK.

YOU WOULD GIVE YOUR LIFE TO HELP THEM. AND SO YOU SHALL. YOUR BLOOD COMPELS YOU.

MUST HAVE FELT A RESIDUAL BUZZ OF THE BLOOD CONTROL, MIND. THE TARDIS BROUGHT ME HERE, AND MY SUBCONSCIOUS MAYBE – JUST MAYBE – PUSHED ME TO CHECK OUT WHAT WAS GOING ON –

THEN IT HAS PUSHED YOU TO YOUR DEATH!

ARRRRRGH!

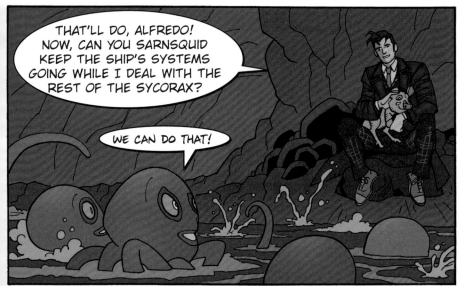

THAT'LL DO, ALFREDO! NOW, CAN YOU SARNSQUID KEEP THE SHIP'S SYSTEMS GOING WHILE I DEAL WITH THE REST OF THE SYCORAX?

WE CAN DO THAT!

OI! BIG FELLA! I PROBABLY COULD DO WITH SOME BACK-UP . . .

OINK!

YOU TOO! WHERE WOULD I BE WITHOUT MY WING-PIG?

OH, CLASSIC SYCORAX! THEY'RE AS MUCH SMOKE-AND-MIRRORS AS BLOOD AND BONE. SHE CONJURED UP A FAKE ARMY, JUST TO INTIMIDATE ME.

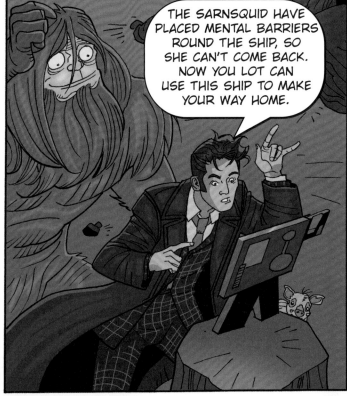

THE SARNSQUID HAVE PLACED MENTAL BARRIERS ROUND THE SHIP, SO SHE CAN'T COME BACK. NOW YOU LOT CAN USE THIS SHIP TO MAKE YOUR WAY HOME.

TIME I WAS OFF TOO. STUFF TO DO

SNORT!

BUT THE SYCORAX ARE STILL OUT THERE. THERE'LL BE A RECKONING. ONE DAY. TIL THEN, LET'S MAKE THE MOST OF SECOND CHANCES . . . SHALL WE?

OINK!

OINK!

THE END.

THE NEXT DOCTOR

Doctor Who showrunner Russell T Davies drops some hints about what the future holds . . .

'Ncuti Gatwa as the Doctor, Millie Gibson as Ruby Sunday, coming to your screens in 2023, *excitement is high.* How lucky am I?'

POLICE TELEPHONE

FREE FOR USE OF PUBLIC

ADVICE & ASSISTANCE OBTAINABLE IMMEDIATELY

OFFICERS & CARS RESPOND TO URGENT CALLS

PULL TO OPEN

DIR DYLAN HOLMES WILLIAMS

DOCTOR WHO

DATE 5th December '22

ROLL # A00 1

'Jemma Redgrave returns as UNIT's Kate Lethbridge-Stewart'

'Also starring Aneurin Barnard as the mysterious Roger ap Gwilliam (ap is Welsh for 'son of', he's not an app. *Or is he?*)'

'Anita Dobson and Michelle Greenidge join us. But what is the significance of the doors . . .?'

THE NEXT DOCTOR

'Back to the 1960s with **Ncuti Gatwa** as the Doctor and **Millie Gibson** as Ruby Sunday! But what's so important about that specific year? What's waiting for the Doctor and Ruby?'

'Jinkx Monsoon as . . . well, who can that be?! SO much fun! So much terror! And not everyone is getting out of this alive . . .'

'Dress to impress and beware the Duchess. Ncuti, Millie and Jonathan Groff as . . . No! Really? But. Whaaat?!?'

PUZZLE ANSWERS

PAGE 18
RANDOM REGENERATIONS

A	14	E	2	I	4	M	1
B	12	F	13	J	3	N	16
C	5	G	6	K	7	O	11
D	8	H	9	L	15	P	10

PAGE 26
DEADLY DIAMOND

```
                              S
                            F I D
                          F D L S N
                        V A V E K G A
                      J W M T N I J W C
                    T V S K S C T A G H L
                  D V F Z W U E H P S E C Y
                N G U F V D A V R O S A S Y Y
              T I L P V S N X R A G V V S A B S
            Q R M H F U G Y V Z M D F E H Y D E U
          A V K I N Z G Z I Y G H M T N W C Q N R C
        D H B J N B D Q U Z J G R P M L U K N S L M L
      N G T B A J D B Q D E L O H F Z Y G O N O W P A V
    P U R C P D X F E O L X F X L K X H K K K R T G E N L
  H D E M N N I M O N Z N I O P Y H S O V G Y I T N M Q D O
J V P U M M R B Q D N M P S P Z V E O S X O V T I S E A N I K
F N A B H O N A N N P W S D E Z U C A N T C Z N E V J U G L B F T
K P E P W D R I K R M H E S K M J V W I T R D I M E Q H U A D I E F E
W S R R V K C A V S K A V X S Q P J K Y F A B R J E V T I R B L F G O A R
M A I A B V H R X H A D N F F M X T S I L C R Q H Q U H Z C M T U P Z O M W I
M E Q V A H H B R K H G C D J X O L Y U M H E A D O J G R A N D S E R P E N T U L
I S Y L T J Y C K D N V Y Y R W N H M C N O E H N U J Z Z M O E L F S Q P A W D V J E
V J G X C Y C L P G R O J X Q E U Q X E H A E K F T H E M E E P O M V B D M G A K B P M P
J W G A S A B Z O R B A L O F F L A X W X I U J P U G H S E W K S M I L E R M H E K C P E B T
G P X B Z K Q N Z S H O R N W G M P M S S L L N T K K N S Y Y S Z T E S H A L S L E G G U X U E I
W G S Q Z U H I C E W A R R I O R J A N S E V D K F A E G C U I Z Z R M Q W O A A L B N Q Z L V Q T L
I W R A R T H W A R R I O R L N T B S G K Q M C O Z T L F A R F Y I A I M Y D R N A M I R E I S K
J C R E T U M E O A X Q S O N F D N T A N D Z R Q W Y O V R E Q T K N B U Y W S K H T R G D O
U C S Y C O R A X N J H K O U A G G E A L N E R Q T Z A E R U O S P F P C U P N V R N D Y
H Z Q X H T N O N U I H E G M Q E R R C V T J B P C C X C I V T E T R A P U F O I O U
D N P U V T K F G S S N Q P H D H M N F O U O V M M T K Z O O F V N S I Q P T O T
O C R U B H A A Q I T N T L S Q A J F L O O D C J L U C R N R P D S Y C P C E
L A S W L A Q P O R I E I O L Q F W D X U I C E F C T E Z I Y S A Z N Q H
E X A S X E Q M L N Y U N A K E B K A S A A V I N B R M F T A N L M T
L O T E O M S W G M B L Z V A T R A X I S E K Q U R U N X E D Y C
D W U H L O M P L Q E M L N Q X E A D I P O S E Y C M T S R N
O F T Z S V B T U X A H W M S Y K S G A O J A Y M V U M A
S Q K R H O I X E T Y I Q O C F J N K S I D J Z N F I
T L W A S R J T H I J A R I A N Z G L N E N S R
O K X Y C E Q U Y Z K B J I H A U P Z N Y R U
C E Y G F B V A S H T A N E R A D A L U L
L U W X E J N S E A D E V I L T H K I
A S Z O M F V G U I A C R I W L S
F O E X Y N Q H P D Y L S H L
A X H J U D O O N L G G Z
N V P Y M Y Q I G X K
E K Y W K R E F F
X Y G K R S R
V W D I D
Z J L
G
```

PAGE 44
DOUBLE DANGER

B2	D3
B3	D4
C2	E1
C3	G3

TO BE
CONTINUED

WITH
NCUTI GATWA
AS THE DOCTOR
AND
MILLIE GIBSON
AS RUBY SUNDAY